Bitza

BOOKS BY ANDREW DADDO

Bitza Series

Bitza

Rules What Rules?

(Illustrated by Stephen Michael King)

Atticus Van Tasticus Series

Atticus Van Tasticus

The Map of Half Maps

The Treasure of Treasures

(Illustrated by Stephen Michael King)

Stuff Happens Series

Ned

Picture Books

Poo Face

Fart Face

(Illustrated by Jonathan Bentley)

Bitza

Andrew Daddo

illustrated by

Stephen Michael King

PENGUIN BOOKS

PENGUIN BOOKS

UK | USA | Canada | Ireland | Australia
India | New Zealand | South Africa | China

Penguin Random House Australia

Penguin Random House Australia is part of the Penguin Random House group of companies whose addresses can be found at global.penguinrandomhouse.com.

First published by Penguin, an imprint of
Penguin Random House Australia Pty Ltd, in 2026

Cover and internal design by Tony Palmer
© Penguin Random House Australia Pty Ltd
Typesetting by Midland Typesetters, Australia

Printed and bound in Australia by Griffin Press, an accredited
ISO AS/NZS 14001 Environmental Management Systems printer

NATIONAL LIBRARY OF AUSTRALIA
A catalogue record for this book is available from the National Library of Australia

MIX
Paper | Supporting responsible forestry
FSC www.fsc.org FSC® C018684

ISBN 978 1 76 135597 4 (Paperback)

We at Penguin Random House Australia acknowledge that Aboriginal and Torres Strait Islander peoples are the Traditional Custodians and the first storytellers of the lands on which we live and work. We honour Aboriginal and Torres Strait Islander peoples' continuous connection to Country, waters, skies and communities. We celebrate Aboriginal and Torres Strait Islander stories, traditions and living cultures; and we pay our respects to Elders past and present.

For Jas, Bibs and Fels. AD

For Chilli, Luka and Willow. SMK

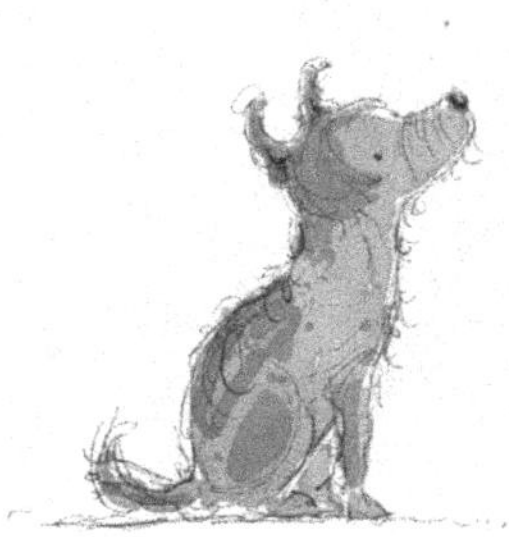

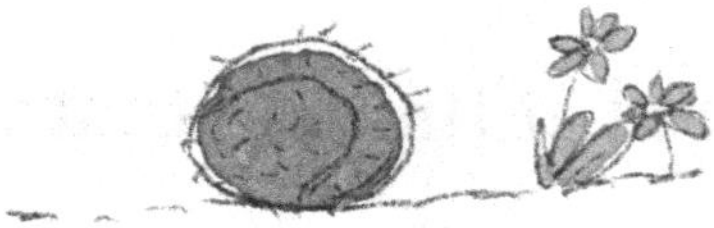

CHAPTER 1

'And who have we got here?' The girl was all bent down and looking at me. First one eye, then the other.

'**That's my ball,**' I went.

'You're a bit of a cutey, you are?' She rubbed my ears and gave me a little rumble under the chin.

It felt nice.

I looked at the dog that was panting on the other side of her legs, the one with my ball in its mouth. Then I looked back at the girl. I couldn't have been clearer if I wanted to be. '**That dog behind**

you is slobbering on my ball.' It was like she couldn't hear me.

'I've never seen a dog like you before. What are you? You look a bit Staffy and a bit Kelpie. I think I can see a bit of Labrador and some doodle, too. You got some doodle in you, eh? Have you got a bit of oodley-doodley?' Her voice was up and sing-songy.

'**It's Poodle,**' I went, thinking everyone forgets oodle is short for Poodle. '**But what I want is my ball.**'

'You really are bits of everything.' She rubbed my ears again, harder this time. It felt *amazing*. 'You're a Bitza, you are.'

I jerked my head up and felt my tail start doing circles. How did she know my name?

'Bits o' this and bits o' that, eh? G'day, Bitza.'

Who's calling who 'Bitza'? I thought. She looked like a bit of a girl and a bit of a boy to me. A bit dark at the top and bit light at the ends. Hair a bit long at the back and a bit short at the front. A bit suntanned and a bit freckly. A bit croaky and a bit squeaky. A bit of everything.

'**G'day, Bitza,**' I went back to the girl. '**Can I have my ball now? Please?**'

The dog behind her had dropped onto its guts and was now licking the ball. *My* ball. I made a quick move towards it but the gristle-haired thing picked it up again, letting its tongue hang out the side of its mouth. *Classy*, I thought.

The girl rubbed my neck and said something about me not having a collar. 'You a bit lost, Bitza? No tag? No collar? Where do you live, Bitz?' She gave that bit of my back just above my tail a scratch and I nearly lost my mind.

'**I wanna live wherever you live while you do that,**' I went. My back leg started to scratch away at nothing at all, even though I tried to stop it.

Then the girl suddenly looked at her watch and gasped. 'Holy cow, we've got to go, Freddy. We're late.'

The dog behind her stood up, stopped panting and squinted its already squinty eyes at me.

'**Ball, thanks,**' I went.

Freddy, if that was the dog's name, shook its head.

'Got to go, Bitza. You're a beautiful dog.' As she said it, she squatted in front of me and rubbed my ears again before holding them up, high and wide, smiling. 'You got some Blue Heeler in you, too? Is that what I can see? Or maybe that's Cattle Dog. Boy you're a beauty, Bitza. Someone's missing you right now.' She stood up, gave me a final pat on the head and said, 'Let's go, Freddy.'

With that, she turned and headed for somewhere else.

'**My ball!**' I went. '**Come back! That mutt is taking my ball.**' It must have been a bit loud because she stopped and turned.

'You better stay, Bitza. Wait for someone to come and find you.'

I better come and look after my ball, was what I was thinking. I took a few steps towards her. '**It's the Border Collie in me. I'm loyal, can't help it. I've got to take care of my ball.**'

'Stay,' she said.

'**Okay,**' I went. But when she turned, I followed. That Freddy kept looking back but never dropped my ball. So, I kept following.

She'd say stay, and I'd stop.

And when she turned to go, I followed.

It went on like that for ages.

Stay.

Follow.

Stop.

Stay.

Follow.

Freddy hung on to my ball.

I hung on to the sight of them.

'You can't come home with me, Bitza.'

'I can,' I went. **'A good dog never leaves their ball behind.'**

Stop.

Stay.

Follow.

'Alright, you might as well come then,' she said. 'Come on, hurry up, Bitza.'

We walked for ages, but I would've gone further. She was chatting away, sometimes to Freddy. Sometimes to me. 'Freddy's a Scottish Terrier, Bitza. Stubborn. Like a chocolate stain on a school shirt. Aren't you, Freddy? Stubborn like rain on a cricket day when it's my turn to bat, you are.' She bent for the ball, but Freddy easily sidestepped her. 'He's alright,' she laughed.

We got to a white fence and Freddy

started to slow down a bit. 'Here you are, Freddy. Home now.' She opened the gate and Freddy went in at a trot. 'Hang on, you goose,' she laughed. I've got to unclip you or you'll get your lead tangled up with your shadow.'

Freddy stopped and waited, one eye on the girl, the other on me.

'There. All good?' She looped the lead around the fence paling and closed the gate, leaving Freddy on the inside.

'**He's got my ball,**' I went, looking up at her with the biggest, saddest Bloodhound eyes I could muster.

'See you, Freddy,' she said, and started walking.

I looked at Freddy through the fence palings. He looked back at me, then dropped the ball and started smiling. I could see it in his eyes before he curled the corners of his mouth.

'**_You'd better go,_**' he went.

'Come on, Bitza, we're nearly home,' the girl said.

I looked that Scottish Terrier Freddy right in the mush and told him, '**That's my ball.**'

Freddy nodded, picked it up, and practically skipped to his front door.

'**Do the right thing, and look after it,**' I called after him. He never looked back.

'Come on, Bitza,' said the girl. 'This is my place.'

She was standing inside the gate, holding it open, the light behind bouncing joy off her head as if it was the sun itself. 'In you come, Bitz.' She tapped the side of her leg and I ran towards her – inside her gate and into her front yard, through her front door and all the way to her back door. When she caught up, Jas opened it and I bolted outside. The smells. The *smells*! She raced after me and tackled me in her very own backyard.

'Geez, I hope no one comes looking for you,' she said as she hugged me hard around the neck.

'**Geez, I hope you're right,**' I went.

She smelt like home.

CHAPTER 2

'Now that I've got you, what am I going to do with you?' She had her hands on her hips and her head tilted to one side. 'I'll bet you're hungry. Stay here.' With that, she turned and went inside.

Of course I followed.

I only got as far as the flyscreen door which gave me a nice little whack in the side of the head as it slammed closed.

'You'd better stay outside,' she said. 'Just in case.'

I could see her fiddling about through the door. There was a bowl and a box and a bottle and some mixing going on. I was pretty sure I knew what she was up to, so I scratched at the flyscreen to let her know I was excited.

'No, Bitz!' she went. 'Don't do that.'

I scratched at it again, as if to say, *What?*

'That!' she said, rushing towards the door with the bowl and slopping stuff on the floor. 'Don't do *that*.'

She opened the door. I went in as she came out. By the time I turned to follow her, the door was on its way back in and gave me another knock on the head.

I'd work it out eventually.

'Silly dog,' she laughed. 'You've got to be careful of the flyscreen. It's on a spring, so it shuts by itself. I bet you thought it was a magic door, didn't you?' She knelt down on the deck and rubbed my head as if it hurt, and that's when I got a half decent whiff of the bowl she'd put down beside her. Milk and something else. Yum.

'Sit,' she said. 'Manners, you know.'

I sat.

'Good Bitza.' She smiled, before putting her hand out. 'High five?'

It looked like an invitation, so I put my paw in hers and let her hang on.

'Oh, you are a clever dog, aren't you? Yes, you are. I bet you can do the other side, too. I bet you can.'

Her voice was up and all sing-songy again. She dropped my paw and put her other hand out, so I did the same, dunking my other foot into her new hand.

I'd been down this road a million times.

'Oh, very good, Bitza,' she practically squealed. 'Got any other tricks?'

Of course I had other tricks, not that I could remember any of them – not with that bowl of milky goodness so close.

Just so you know, it's not as if I have any say in whether drool stays in or comes out of my mouth. It's the hound in me – though I'm not really sure what kind of hound that is. I do know that I can smell very well. And when I smell food, I tend to drool. It just happens. It's like someone turns on a tiny drool tap in my mouth and eventually it fills up and spills out the corners. Right side first, then left. It's not a problem – for me.

'You're starving, aren't you,' she said. 'Sorry, Bitza. Here you go.'

She put the bowl on the deck, and I got amongst it. It was cold and mushy and milky and beautiful while it lasted. The way I can make food disappear is definitely one of my better tricks.

'Oh, my goodness,' she laughed. 'That was amazing. And probably a bit disgusting, Bitza.' When she picked up the bowl, I cleaned up the mess I'd made on the deck. 'You want more?' she asked.

'Well, duh! That's like asking if cats are a little creepy? I'm part Labrador, of course I want more!'

'Wait here,' she said. Jas went inside and I waited for as long as I could before following. I almost made it, this time copping the flyscreen door in the neck. I really would get the better of that door eventually.

'Stay, Bitz,' she said again, but she'd opened the floodgates on my hunger, and I scratched at the flyscreen hard enough to leave a scrape. 'Bitza, no!' she went, then opened the door for me so I could come in. *That was easy*, I thought.

'No scratching the door, Bitz.' She sounded stressed so I gave her the sad eyes and sat. 'You're a good dog. I can see it. But don't scratch at the door.'

'**I won't,**' I lied.

She was halfway to a cupboard when there was a new noise at the other end of the house.

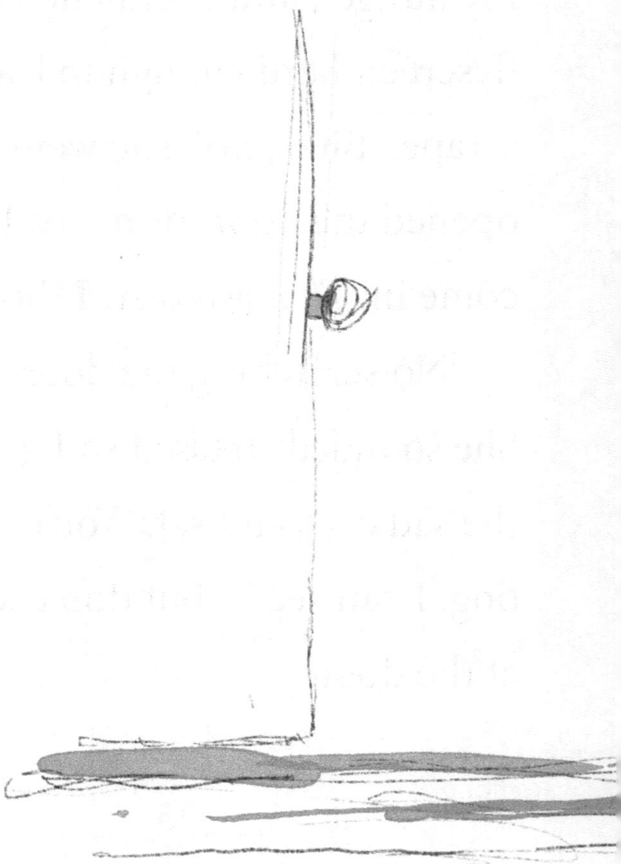

A key in the door maybe?

Door opening? Big footsteps?

Then a new voice.

'Jas?'

Definitely a new voice. A big one.

'Jas, you home? Can you give me a hand?'

'Oh my gosh, Bitz. It's Dad. You have to hide.'

CHAPTER 3

Things happened pretty fast.

The bowl of food was left on the bench.

Jas stepped quickly out of the kitchen and backed through a couch room into a doorway and started making faces at me. Her face looked like she was yelling but her mouth was making tiny noises. 'Come 'ere, Bitza. Bitz. Come here!' She was waving with both hands. 'Please come here!'

There were more sounds further up the house.

A door closing.

The clank of something being dropped. A grumble, a door being opened again, a scrape and a thump and a door going bang. Then not much at all.

I was still in the kitchen watching Jas but listening to whatever it was making the new noises.

'Come here, Bitza.' She was a little louder, but no less stressed.

I looked at the bowl on the edge of the bench. I wondered if I could reach it if I stood up on my back legs. Jas came running back into the kitchen and grabbed at me, pulling

in the direction she'd just come from. 'Come on, Bitz. Let's go!'

She took me to the room she'd been in and closed the door.

Wow.

What a glorious, fantastic mess.

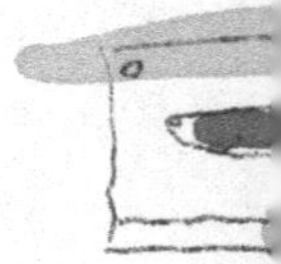

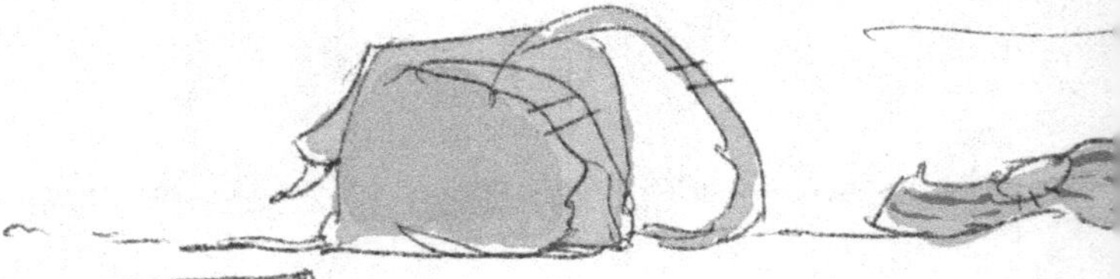

Such a room. What smells. It was like walking into a whole world of Jas.

There were clothes everywhere. And a bed. And toys. Two footies, a soccer ball and all sorts of shoes. There were even dog pictures on the wall.

'My dad's home, Bitz. I'll have to hide you. Where will you fit?' She was looking around, doing circles, a bit like a dog looking for a spot to poo. 'Under the bed?'

My drool tap was leaking. No matter how many times I swallowed, I could feel it starting to pool in the sides of my mouth.

I watched her lift the doona to look under the bed. No chance I'd fit down there, even though it looked like a great place to hang out. I barked. A good one. It was my way of letting her know that was never going to work.

She flipped. 'Shhhhh,' she went, her index finger up to her mouth. 'Bitza, shhhhhh!'

I loved that she called me Bitza.

'Why are you slobbering?' Jas whispered.

I just looked at her with my hungry eyes. '**It's the food. You left the bowl of food in the kitchen.**'

'You have to be quiet, like a mouse. There's no way Dad'll let you stay. He hates dogs.'

'**What?**' I went, cocking my head to one side so she could see how confusing that idea really was.

Then I cocked it the other way, hard enough to flop my ear onto the top of my head. '**Arooooooo.**'

'Bitza!' She made a face, a bit like the face a fish might make when it chomps on a hook and realises it's caught.

'**Who hates dogs?**' I sat on my backside and looked at her, trying to work out if she was worried or excited. There were footsteps from somewhere else, and they were getting louder.

'Good boy for sitting, Bitza, now shhhhhh,' she whispered, but quietly this time. She gently rubbed the top of my head while holding a finger to her mouth.

'So you *are* home, Jas.' There was a little knock on the door. 'When did you get in, I was looking for some help with the groceries?'

'Oh, sorry, Dad. I didn't hear you.' Jas's face changed as she watched the doorknob slowly turn. 'Hang on, Dad. I'm getting changed.' As she said it, she made an eeeeek face, shaking her head.

'Yeah, righto,' went the deep voice from outside the door. 'Dinner's on soon. Have you got homework? You might want to get to it, the footy's on tonight. I thought we could watch it together.'

'Sounds good.' She didn't sound like it sounded good. The footsteps started up again, going from loud to quiet to nothing at all. 'That was a close one, Bitz.'

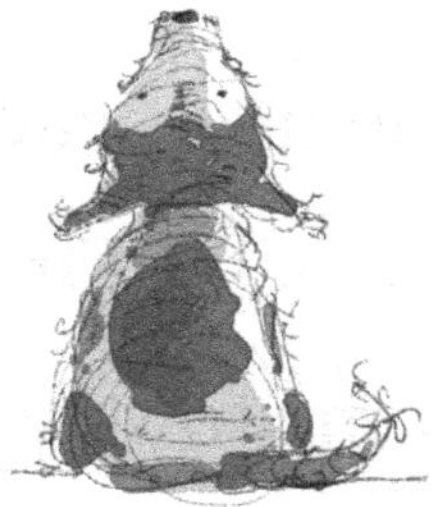

CHAPTER 4

Jas put her hands on her hips and looked at me. 'We have to hide you.'

On the bed, under the doona, I thought. *It's perfect. I'll stay there forever.* I jumped up to show her how easily I fit the bed. It was beautiful, like a couch but flatter.

She jumped onto the bed next to me and got me in a headlock. 'You can't hide here, silly. Or wait, can you?' Jas told me to stay still while she covered me with cushions and a blanket, leaving just my face clear. 'Stay,' she said. 'Don't move. Stay.'

I stayed.

She went to the door and looked back. 'I can barely see you. It's like a pile of cushions and

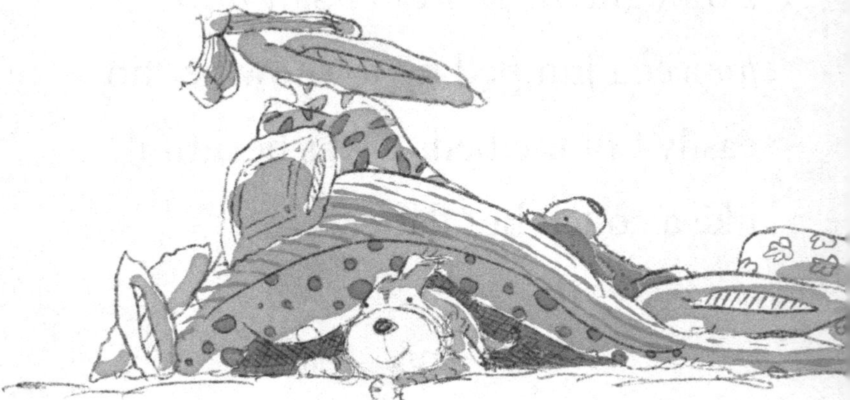

your face is kind of like a dog cushion. No offence.'

None taken, I thought.

That's where you have to hide. It's there or the wardrobe. She pointed at a door in the wall.

I didn't want to go in the wardrobe.

'You stay there, okay? I'll come back soon. Then you can have some more food.'

Foooooood. The slobber tap was back in the ON position.

'Good dog, stay there.' She opened the door to her room, walked out and just before she closed it, stuck her head back in. 'Shhhhhh, okay?'

'**Arrooooo!**' I went. '**Of course.**'

'Bitza!'

'**Rrrroooooer.**'

She came back into the room, closing the door behind her. 'Shhhhhhhh.'

I went '**Rrrrrrrrr,**' as in, 'got it'.

'Bitz!'

I sat up. Cushions spilled off the bed. I stood up but stayed low because she was obviously up for a game.

'Stop.'

'**What?**'

'Shhhhhh.'

'Who shoosh?' It wasn't Jas that said it. It was from outside the room, then the doorknob turned and a big man's face peered around the door. 'Who are you shooshing, Jassy?'

I froze on the bed.

Jas closed her eyes tight as if she was hiding. She didn't turn around to look at the man at the door.

'Jasper. There's a dog on your bed.'

'Where, Dad?' she said, slowly turning to look at her father.

'There. Sitting in the middle of your bed. I'm pretty sure that's a dog,' he said. He didn't sound cross. He slowly came all the way into the room and made a come here sign to Jasper. 'Slowly, now, Jas. Come here, out of your room. There is a dog on your bed.'

'I know,' she said. Instead of walking to her dad, she backed up towards me. 'I found him. His name's Bitza.'

'Oh,' was all he said.

'He's beautiful, don't you think?'

Dad raised an eyebrow and lowered his chin at me. 'He's got to go home, is what I think.'

I am home, is what *I* was thinking.

'He is home,' Jas said, sitting on the bed and rubbing her hand on my back.

‘Don’t touch it,’ said Dad. ‘You don’t know what it’s got.’

Excuse me, very much.

‘Jas, out. Dog, out. Everyone out. Now!’

I knew a pack leader when I heard one. I jumped off the bed and bolted, looking for somewhere else to be.

Jas wasn’t far behind me. ‘You’ve scared him, Dad. You scared Bitza.’

‘Jas, wait.’

I headed straight for the flyscreen door, but it was shut, so I scratched at it. Once. Twice. Then up on my back legs to give it a proper wrestle. It didn't budge, but it would have if I'd kept at it.

Jas caught up to me and opened the door. I went straight out and into the backyard, where I stayed.

Jasper stuck her head out the door and whispered, 'Stay there, Bitza. It'll be fine. Don't go anywhere!'

I definitely wasn't going anywhere because I had nowhere to go. Not really. '**Arooor,**' I hounded.

'Jassy. We need to talk about the dog,' Jasper's dad said.

I heard it as plain as a tom cat's meow. It didn't sound good. Like, he wasn't going to let me sleep on the bed, put it that way.

But then, maybe he *did* want me to sleep on the bed. Maybe that's just how he sounded.

Stranger things had happened.

CHAPTER 5

I stayed on the deck and watched as hard as I listened. Jas and her dad came into the kitchen and sat on stools at the bench. I couldn't hear what they were saying, but she was nodding, and he was shaking his head. Then she was shaking her head, and he was nodding.

Then she looked like she was crying.

He looked like he was sorry but kept shaking his head.

She covered her face so I couldn't tell what was going on. He got up, moved to the other side of the bench and picked up the bowl I'd had a bit of feed from earlier. He smelt it, then shook his head, as if to say, 'Hot dang, that is some good smelling tucker'. Jas looked up then took the bowl from him and went to the back door.

'Bitza.'

I didn't have to be asked twice.

'Watch this, Dad.' She came out the flyscreen door and I backed up a bit to give her some room. Her dad followed her out.

'Bitza, sit.'

I sat.

'High five?'

I looked at her, then her dad. Back to Jas. She still had her hand out for me to shake, the bowl of food was in her other hand.

'High five, Bitz?'

You bet.

'Other hand?' She swapped the food bowl into her other hand. Even though I would have loved to dive on that food, I high-fived the hand I was meant to. The dribble tap was running. I could feel it.

'See, Dad? See? He's really smart.'

Dad had his arms folded and was hanging back a bit. 'Can you drop, Bitza?'

'**Like this?**' I went, lying flat on the ground.

Dad unfolded his arms and squatted down in front of me. 'Sit up, mate,' he said, sounding a little warmer.

I sat. Drool broke the banks of my gums and headed for the ground. It was thick juicy slobber. Good quality stuff.

'Give him the bowl, Jas. Quick.'

She put the bowl of food in front of me, and it was easily as good as the bowl before.

I didn't mind that they watched me eat, as long as they didn't want me to share it. Besides, I watch people eat all the time. I watch them and go up to them. I put my head on

their knees or tap them with my feet. I love watching people eat almost as much as I love eating.

'He's a bit of alright, isn't he?' said Dad.

'A *bit* of alright? Dad, he's beautiful.'

I looked up at the two of them. Both with their arms folded, one foot pointed at me, the other foot pointed to the side. The two of them had their heads ever so slightly to one side. Jas was smiling, Dad wasn't. Then he said, 'Someone's missing him for sure.'

CHAPTER 6

Jas slid an arm around her dad's waist. 'Can he sleep in my room?'

'We've got to find his home, Jas.'

'Where's your home, Bitz?' Jas said to me. And even though I was thinking, *it feels like it's here*, I didn't say anything.

‘No collar?’

‘Nup.’

Dad squatted in front of me and told me to sit. I sat. He grabbed my face in both hands and gave me a really great rub. He was rough and strong, and it felt amazing, like a scratch above the tail, only better. He looked in one ear, then the other. ‘No tattoos,’ he said.

I pulled my head away and looked at him. ‘**Of course not,**’ I said, shaking my head and getting my ears back into shape. ‘**I'm probably more Poodle than**

Pitbull, you know? Tatts aren't really my thing.'

'Maybe he's been microchipped.'

'Micro-what?' said Jas, squatting down and giving me a pat on the head.

'It's a little electronic chip they put into dogs so they can be identified.

It's a good way to find the owner. Lots of dogs have them. We just have to take him to the pound, and they'll scan him and find out where he lives.'

Pound? I'd heard that word but couldn't remember where.

Jas tickled me under the chin. 'If we take him to the pound, they'll keep him, won't they? They'll keep him and hold him and if no one turns up they'll – Dad, you know what they do to dogs at the pound!' I could hear the tears behind her eyes way before they spilled out the front. 'No pound, Dad.'

'He can't stay here, Jas. He's someone else's dog. As happy as you are to have him here, there's someone else who's going to be very, very sad not to have him there. At his home. In front of his fire or in his kennel or wherever he sleeps.'

'**I can sleep here,**' I went. '**It'd be pretty good here, I'd reckon.**'

'Why can't he stay?' She had me hug-locked and it was great.

'Cos he's not our dog.'

'But he could be.'

'**Yeah, I could be,**' I arooored.

He stood up, put his hands on his hips and blew a long breath out of his mouth. A big, thinking kind of breath. 'Jas. Honey. Come on. We don't have room for a dog. Or the time. *Definitely* not the time. You know that.'

She looked around the kitchen and living room, then stood up, put her arms out wide and did a little spin. Then she went outside and did the same thing in the middle of the deck. Then again, in the middle of the grass in the

backyard. I ran behind twirling with her.

As she walked back in through the door she said, 'Dad, seriously. We have heaps of room for a dog. There's more room here than at Freddy's place and he's happy as.'

'He's happy because you walk him.'

'And I'll walk Bitza, too.'

'Of course you will. I bet you'll clean up his poop, as well. You'll water the lawn after he pees on it so we don't end up with yellow circles all over the place.

You'll feed him and walk him and wash him and all that stuff. Until you won't. Then I'll have to do it.' He folded his hands across his chest and looked a little sad.

It made Jas look a bit sad, too.

What if I don't pee on the lawn? I thought, but they couldn't hear me thinking. Instead, I went over to Dad and put my paw on his knee.

'Oh, look at that, Dad. He loves you!'

'He wants more food,' Dad said.

'**That, too.**' I went. '**But I'll try not to wee on the lawn if**

it's a dealbreaker. Honestly. I'll really try.'

Dad reached down and rubbed my head, getting the knuckles in that groove right in the middle of my ears, making my back leg shake. Then he reached down with his other hand and grabbed my whole head, pulling his face close to mine and having a proper look at me.

It let me have a proper look at him, too. He had a nice face. Kind eyes, a few smiley wrinkles and little bags under there, nothing a decent night's sleep wouldn't fix. And he smelt good, like the earth was in him, like he was a digger, too.

He dropped his head and shut his eyes. 'Oh, Jassy,' he whispered as much to me as to her.

He stayed like that until I tapped his foot with mine. With a wipe of his nose, he looked up and sounded serious. 'Take a photo of him. We'll make a flyer and put them around the place tomorrow. That's as good as I can do. We'll wait until Monday and if no one comes along, then we're going to the pound. It's that or nothing, okay?'

She went over to him and wrapped her arms around his neck, planting a big fat kiss on the side of his face. 'We're gonna keep him, aren't we, Dad? You're the best!'

'We're going to find his family, that's what we're going to do.'

'Sure, Dad,' she said, letting him go and turning to me. 'Unless he's already found his family.'

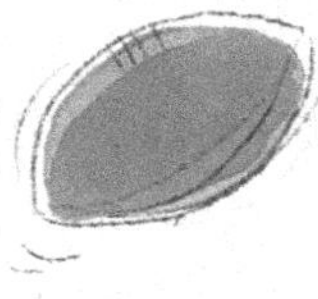

CHAPTER 7

'Okay? Anything else?' Jas was at the computer, turning her face this way and that. Her dad was behind her. Frowning.

He pointed at the computer screen. 'Don't you think you should add a photo as well?'

'Oh, duh,' she laughed. There was some tapping and some more head tilting and then she said she was done. 'Print?'

'Print!' he said.

A piece of paper slid out of a box on the desk. Dad picked it up and the two of them looked at it. 'I suppose it's alright,' he said.

'It's perfect,' she said, then turned the page around for me to see. There were some scribbles, and a very small picture of something, maybe a dog, at the top of the poster.

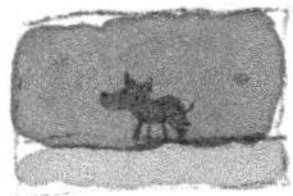

Dog Found

In Ivanhoe's Park

Friday Night.

Call 049 855 300

if you know where he lives.

Dad leaned over Jas and started tapping at the computer. 'Or we could use this one.'

A whirring at the box before a new page slid out. Jas grabbed it and stared for a while. Then looked back at the first page. 'Mine's better,' she said, then showed me both pages.

The second page had a much bigger picture of the dog, which looked strangely familiar, and some smaller scribble below it.

'Nope,' Dad said. 'Mine's better, and that's the one we're going to use.'

The printer went to work and soon enough there was a small stack of posters ready to go up around the neighborhood. 'First thing tomorrow, we hit the streets.

We'll hit the park, the cafe, the supermarket and maybe even the vet, what do you say?'

Jas looked at me first, then her dad. 'I say it's a waste of time because no one is going to make Bitza any happier than me.' She hugged me hard around the neck which made it tough to lick her face, but I tried anyway. She did make me very happy. 'But, okay, we can give it a go.'

'Great,' went Dad.

'We'll see,' went Jas.

'Who'd you tip in the footy?' he said.

‘Doggies,’ said Jas. ‘Every time. Want to watch the footy, Bitz?’ she said, taking off for her room.

I stayed where I was, not sure if I should follow. When she came out, she was holding a footy, moving it about as if she wanted me to grab it. I was so excited I nearly peed.

‘Easy, Tiger,’ went Dad. ‘Don’t tease him. And don’t get too fond of him, who knows what’s going to happen tomorrow.’

Jas stopped playing with the ball, tucking it under her arm. ‘Hmmmm,’ she went. ‘But I do

know what's happening tonight. You,' she said, pointing at me, 'are sleeping with me.'

CHAPTER 8

'Don't tell Dad, but I've accidentally on purpose put way too much cereal in my bowl and you can eat what I can't.' She winked at me after she said it, then set about eating whatever was in the bowl. She's a slurper. Sluuuuuuurrrps from the spoon is what she does, then crunches whatever gets left behind. I was sitting right in front of her, watching.

Crunch. Crunch. Crunch. 'Did you love sleeping on my bed more than anything in the whole world?' she asked through half a mouthful.

I dropped my head onto her knee as if to say, *You know I did!*

There'd been a bit of a tussle between Jas and her dad. He said I had to sleep outside, she said there was no way I could because I didn't have anywhere to sleep. She said it was inhuman. He said I was not human so that was okay. She said very funny, right before he said ha ha. Then he said, at least put a blanket or something on the bed so the dog doesn't leave hair everywhere. She told him she loved him, and he looked like he was going to melt.

There was a stack of food left in her bowl for me.

I made a mess of it and cleaned it up and got a 'good boy' for my troubles.

'Dad,' yelled Jasper. 'Daaaad? Where's the sticky tape?'

No answer.

'Daaaaaaaaaaad?' She was in the third drawer down in the kitchen, moving stuff around. 'Dad, the sticky?' But there was still no answer. She went up a drawer and fished about in there. 'I know the sticky tape is here somewhere.'

But it wasn't. Not in any of the drawers, or the cupboard by the door or anywhere near the printer.

But then there was the sound of the front door opening, and something landing on the hall table, and the door closing, followed by big, heavy footsteps pounding down the hall. It was him. Top Dog.

'Oh, good,' he puffed. 'You haven't gone yet.' He was holding a paper bag which he put on the bench. 'Good morning, Mr Bitz, good morning, Miss Jasper. I found something you might like.' He fished around in the bag and pulled out some sticky tape. 'For the shop windows and the gate at the park. Aaaaaaand,' he said theatrically. 'I thought you might need one of these.' It was a bright blue collar. 'And one of these.' A bright blue lead that perfectly matched the collar. 'And some of these.'

I knew that smell and the packet wasn't even open. It was dog treats. Probably kangaroo but possibly regular beef.

Jas was busy tearing at the packaging for the collar.

'And last, but not least,' Dad said, 'a ball to chase. For fun. At the park. I'm guessing all dogs like balls.'

'**No!**' I yelled. '**All dogs don't like balls, we LOVE them! Aroooooooooooooooo!**' I went.

'You're the best, Dad,' said Jas.

'I know,' he said, then laughed.

CHAPTER 9

We put the posters up all over the place, which Jas didn't love, but Dad said we had to. In lots of shop windows. On bus stops. On poles at the park and in the street and even down by the beach. There were posters on picnic tables and letter boxes and phone booths and finally, after Dad had talked to the vet, in the vet window.

The vet even came out and looked at me. He gave me a pat and something chewy and looked at my teeth and my ears before shaking his head. He said, 'He's beautiful, and he's healthy, but he's not one of mine.'

Jas did a fist pump.

I hoped for another chewy.

Dad taped a poster inside the window and said thanks.

On the way home, we went back to the park and had a throw around with the ball. It was pretty much one of the best days ever.

First Jas held up the ball and asked me if I was ready. *Oh yes, was I ready*!

Then Dad grabbed a stick and said, 'Are you sure you don't want the stick?'

'Of course I want the stick,' I went, moving a little closer to him.

'Or do you want the ball, Bitza? Does Bitza want the ball?' She was tossing it from hand to hand and talking to me like she was singing.

'Of course I want the ball.'

'Or the stick?' Dad moved closer to Jas, so now they were standing

side-by-side. They were looking at each other and laughing, saying 'stick' and 'ball' and waving them around.

'**Both!**' I wanted to yell. '**Throw both!**'

When Jas put the ball behind her back, Dad said, 'So, now do you want the stick?'

'**Of course I want the stick.**'

'But not the ball?' said Jas.

'**Yes, I want the ball, but I can't see it anymore. I'll have the stick because I can see it.**'

Jas bent down and held the ball out to me. My lip started to quiver, the drool building in my mouth.

'Which one?' they said together, Jas with the ball, Dad with the stick.

If I opened my mouth to answer, there'd be a slobber tsunami. So, just using my eyes, I said, '**The ball is always my first choice. It's always been like that. I mean, balls can be kicked or bounced or rolled or** even slobbered on. It's like they have a life of their own. I can drop a ball on a hill and it'll roll away from me. I wait. I watch. I pretend someone like you has just thrown it, then I run and get it. But balls are always more fun with someone like you to play with.'

Dad and Jas just stared at me.

I guess they want to know about the stick, I thought.

'A stick is cool, too. But you can't roll a stick. You can chew it until it's just mess all over the place. And you can wrestle other dogs for a stick, play tug of war, get wood stuck between your teeth. You can even trip someone over with a stick if you can find one long enough. Sticks are great. But they're not balls.'

They both nodded, just as a line of slobber tipped out of my mouth.

'Ready, Dad?' said Jas. 'Three, two, one – you asked for it, Bitza!' And they both threw at the same time.

What a time! WHAT A DAY!

Then we headed for home.

'What do we do now, Dad?' said Jas as I collapsed on the lounge room floor.

As much as I wanted to listen, I could barely keep my eyes open. If he answered, I missed it.

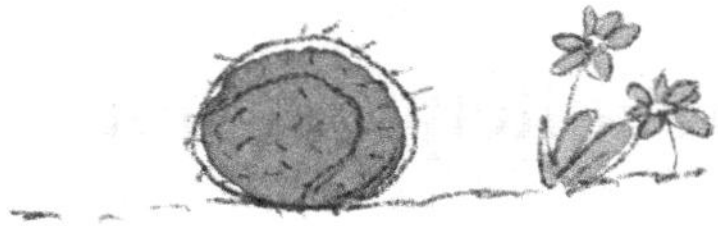

CHAPTER 10

I didn't like the sound I'd woken up to.

It was a sad sound.

I sat up, hoping what I was hearing wasn't what I thought, but it was. Jas was crying.

Dad was talking quietly, and she was nestled into his shoulder.

He rubbed her back which didn't stop it from heaving, and whatever he said definitely was not making her feel any better.

I trotted up and tried to help. First by sitting without being asked, then patting her foot with mine. Jas looked down at me and cried even harder. Between the sobs

she managed, 'Somebody saw the poster and they rang Dad's phone. They're coming over to get you.' But it kind of came out like, 'They are-are-are coming ov-ov-over to get you-oooo-hoohoohoohoooo.'

Trust me, there is nothing sadder in the world than a girl you're falling in love with falling apart.

Then Dad looked down and *he* had tears in his eyes as well. He reached out and patted me roughly on the head, saying, 'Sorry, mate. You'll be home soon.'

Jassy wrestled herself from her father's grip and sat on the ground so she could hug me hard around the neck.

I got up on my back legs and pushed into her, making her fall over backward. She laughed a bit. What a great sound that was.

I went straight for her face, licking for all I was worth. She laughed and

tried to push me away but I kept at it and she kept laughing.

Then there was a knock at the door.

The licking stopped with the laughter.

'No!' was all she said, but I knew it wasn't at me.

Dad bent down and grabbed her hands, gently helping her stand up. 'It'll be okay, Jas. It really will be okay.'

He walked down the hallway but Jas stayed with me. She was down on one knee, with one arm around me, the other rubbing my chest.

The door opened and I knew that smell before it was halfway down the hall. I knew the voice, too.

'Mr Byrne? Hi, I'm Peggie. I called about Fitzy the dog.'

It couldn't be! I broke Jassy's hold and headed for the hall.

'Noooooo,' wailed Jas.

As much as I wanted to turn around, I had to get down the hall and be sure it was her. The sun was bright outside and dark in the hallway, but the smell and the shape and the sound of her voice made me absolutely certain it was her.

When she saw me coming at full gallop she dropped to her knees and said in that sweet, high voice. 'Oh, Fitzy! We were so worried! Where have you been?'

'**I've been here!**' I laughed, jumping up and trying to lick her all over the face. '**Here is where I've been. It's great. This is Dad,**

and that's Jas and we've had the best time ever! Where have you been?'

'Oh, Fitzy,' she said again with a laugh. She rubbed me hard on the ears the way Jas's Dad did and I realised why I'd liked it so much when he did it. 'Fitzy, you funny old dog!'

'So, he is yours,' said Dad. 'Hmmmm. That's good. Good that he's found you.' He gave me a pat as well and shouted out to Jassy. 'Jas, Fitzy's mum is here. You'd better come and say goodbye.'

I looked down the hall and there was Jas, her head poking around the corner. She'd been watching, I could just tell.

She wiped her face with both hands then her T-shirt and slowly started coming down the hall.

'Hi, there,' said Peggy.

Jas stopped halfway down the hall and did a U-turn.

'Are you getting the lead?' said Dad. 'We're not going to need it anymore.'

The lead. I knew what that meant. We were going for a walk! *Better find the ball*, I thought, hotfooting it down the hallway. I was pretty sure I'd left it under the couch. Or outside. Or maybe in her bedroom.

Nope, under the couch, because I'd been playing with it and was a bit sad when I couldn't reach it. Low couches are a dog's worst friend.

'**Arooooo-roooo,**' I went, down on my haunches looking under the couch.

'I'll get it for you, Bitz. Hang on a sec.' Jas got down on her guts and started wriggling under the couch, arm outstretched, trying to knock the ball out for me. Geez she was good.

I could hear them talking up the end of the hall. It was low voices like they were up to something.

The ball got moving and I got after it, getting a good grip and bolting for the front door. Jas was up and about pretty quickly and set out after me.

I love being chased!

'Whoa there, Fitzy. Slow down,' went Peggy. She'd half blocked the door so I couldn't get past. 'You must be Jas,' she said to Jas. 'You found Fitz, I hear.'

Jassy nodded. 'Yep. He was in the park and followed me home.' I could tell from the sound of Jas's voice she was going to cry, so I dropped the ball to try and happy her up. She

picked it up and gave it a wipe on her jeans.

'That was very nice of you to look after him,' said Peggy. 'He's lovely.'

'Why's he called Fitz?' said Dad. 'It seems a funny name for a dog.'

Peggy laughed. 'Yes, it is. But he just fits. He's one of those dogs.

Well, he did fit, anyway. He's my dad's dog . . . *was* my dad's dog, but Dad's no longer with us.' Now she looked so very sad. 'It was all a bit sudden, actually. He loved Fitz, they did everything together. We guessed Fitz took off because he was a bit lost, you know?'

No one said anything.

I sat next to Jas. Nice and straight. She was moving the ball from one hand to the other.

Peggy started talking again. 'So, we've got to find him a home because as much as I want to, I can't look after him. It's got to be a good home, though. A *great* home. A great home for a great boy, eh, Fitz?'

Now Peggy was crying, so I sat in front of her and pawed at her leg.

'Wouldn't know any great homes, would you?'

Dad looked up to the ceiling and blew out a long breath.

'Yes!' said Jas, almost as a squeal. 'Yes, we do know a great home, don't we, Dad?'

Dad sucked his teeth and shook his head. 'Look, um. We, ahhhh. Um, we don't really –'

'Yes, we are a great home, Dad. We *are*. You say it all the time. You say, *This is a great home!*'

'But I don't mean that. I mean –'

'Dad!'

Peggy looked from Dad to Jas and back again. 'I might be getting ahead of things, but I've got his blanket and his water bowl with me. And there's a stack of food for him. You've got a lead and collar already, so his old stuff could be a backup. What do you say? Shall we do a trial? Just see how it goes for a week or so?'

'Yes!' went Jas. 'We can definitely do that.' But Dad wasn't so sure, umming and ahhhing again. 'Dad! Please? Just a trial! Please, Dad.'

'Nup,' he said. And it was a hard *nup*. A 'no more talking, no more begging, we're done' kind of *nup*.

Jas knew it, too. When I looked at her face, her bottom lip started quivering. Dad rubbed her on the head, as if to make it stop.

Peggy looked at me as if to say, *this is not going to work out, Big Fella.*

Then Dad cleared his throat. A big, deep, Dad-ish *Hmm-hmmm.* 'It's nup because . . .' and he let it hang there for ages, '. . . we're not interested in a trial. We're interested in Fitzy staying here forever.'

'What?' bawled Jas. 'WHAT?' She was practically screaming.

'Buuut,' he said, 'there's one condition.'

'Anything,' said Jas.

'Mmmmm?' said Peggy, but it was a pretty happy *Mmmmm.*

Dad smiled. 'The one condition is –'

'**Arooooooooo,**' I went. I mean, come on. Spit it out, Dad.

'The one condition, and it's up to Peggy, is that we can call him Bitz not Fitz. Or Bitza. Would that be okay?'

'**Call me whatever you like,**' I yelled. '**Just don't call me late for dinner!**' It was a joke.

'Dad used to call him Bitz, too.' Peg nodded. 'Sometimes, anyway. Because no one was ever really sure what he was, apart from lovely.

He's a lovely dog, Fitz is. And now he's yours.'

'Dad? Is he really ours?'

'**Are you really mine?**' I arooood.

'Yep. I reckon he is. Welcome home, Bitz,' he said, knuckling me on the top of the head. 'Welcome home.'

Jas threw the ball down the hall, and I took off after it. The ball managed to avoid the stools at the kitchen bench and was bouncing straight for the wire door. If I judged it right, I knew I could jump and get it just before it got there.

I judged it wrong.

The wire in the door wasn't nearly as strong as I thought it was, and I sailed straight through it onto the deck outside.

'Bitza,' yelled Jassy, running down the hall after me.

I knew I had a feeling about this place, and that feeling felt a lot like home.

Fallen in love with Bitza?

Need more adventures? No problem!

OUT NOW!

More Bitza adventures

COMING SOON!!